Mask of the Varza

Nathan Paul

The cultures depicted are fictitious and not meant to depict real-world cultures. However, inspiration has been taken from real-world cultures in the creation of the fictitious cultures in the book.

Book Cover by Alison Keller

First edition 2026

Content Warning: This story contains mature themes and intense sequences that some readers may find distressing including: blood and gore, harm to animals, physical trauma (injury descriptions), depictions of death in battle, themes of fear, shame and isolation, and supernatural horror.

Dedicated to everyone who aided me in the creation of this novella, including my parents Rik Paul and Debi Albeyta, Alison Keller, Yudong Liu, Tara Paul, Hyungjin Park, Barbara McCole and Maryn Paul.

Contents

Chapter 1 1

Chapter 2 4

Chapter 3 7

Chapter 4 11

Chapter 5 18

Chapter 6 21

Chapter 7 25

Chapter 8 30

Chapter 9 34

Chapter 10 39

Chapter 11 43

Chapter 12 47

Chapter 13 50

Acknowledgements 63

About the author 64

Chapter 1

The storyteller's eyes were shut in peaceful repose to excite the cluster of children who cautiously inched forward, awaiting the Shava's next epic tale. A serene, ivory mask hid the rest of his weathered face; tufts of dried grass sprouted from it like hair, and carvings of lions, eagles, fish and horses danced upon its cheeks. Though the time was a little past midday outside, too hot for anyone to work, the tent held an aura of twilight, an illusion reinforced by a menagerie of leather stars and moons that were flecked with bits of sparkling copper and bronze. Small sacks of powders and herbs hung from the tent's ceiling at varying lengths, one of which a bored child prodded.

When the Shava was ready, he did little but open his eyes. It was a slight motion, but the children jumped back in alarm. A few giggled. The bored boy stopped poking the sack. The Storyteller kept his mouth closed, letting his gaze rest on each child, who squirmed when his eyes settled on him or her.

Finally, one bold boy in front spoke up.

"Tell us the tale of Edjeera and the Five Lions, Shava-mei," he ordered. The Shava's masked face remained expressionless, but his eyes were fixed upon the boy. There was a long pause as the children awaited his response. Eventually, he gave it.

"Someone has forgotten the way we do things here," he said, "for that I will not tell the tale of Edjeera and the Five Lions until the next full moon."

The boy sunk back, disappointed and mortified. Half of the children groaned and the other half laughed.

"Cheer up, now. You will one day make a great Varza, but remember that when in the place of the Shava, you must behave in the way of the Shava," the storyteller said.

The boy puffed up his chest at those words.

"That's right," said the boy, "I will be the greatest fighter. I will show no fear."

The storyteller's eyes lingered on the boy, but said nothing. A girl with a split lip spoke up.

"That's a lie! You ran faster than a horse when you saw that snake!"

"Quiet!", the boy jumped to his feet. "I did not! It could have killed me."

He opened his mouth to say more but the storyteller clapped his hands together with such swiftness that it sounded as if a bolt of lightning had burst into the tent. The boy and girl fell silent and all the children turned their attention once more to him.

"Enough," he said softly, for his hands had spoken with the force he needed, "I will have you both thrown out if either of you speaks one word more."

His look lingered on the boy before passing on to the girl.

"There is glory and honor that comes when you receive the mask of a Varza," he said. "You may earn praise, and perhaps stories will be made of your deeds. But the path of Varza is not an easy one. The herds must be cared for and Kourek's walls must be maintained. But, there is also fear that must be conquered. When riding forth to fight the enemies of the Koureki, death and pain ride with you, and such things can make even the greatest Varza feel afraid. But to protect the Koureki people, it must be overcome."

Another girl raised her hand after two hesitant tries, and the storyteller nodded to her.

"But, Shava-mei, in the stories, the greatest Varza don't feel fear. Durukhi doesn't, nor does Gashgha. When Edjeera fought the Five Lions, she never ran from them. I don't understand."

The storyteller stared at her, his eyes partially hidden by the shadows of the mask. The girl shrank in upon herself, fearing that he would cast her from the tent.

"I have decided on a story," he finally said. "I will not speak of Edjeera and the lions, but Edjeera has other stories. Let me tell you of how Edjeera faced her fear."

Chapter 2

Edjeera was born and lived in a good time, when the horses grazed upon grass so green it glowed, when our beans were bloated and fat, when our neighbors were ruled by worthy chiefs and councils who saw the wisdom in peace. She was not a large child when she was born, but she was born to wear the mask of a Varza. When she came out of the womb, she did not shed a tear and instead glared at the delivery woman before giving her a kick in the chin. She did not nurse, she gulped down her milk. But even then, not for long, since she refused to stay still. Her mother was a patient woman, for Edjeera was an explorer and required much supervision to keep her out of trouble. Whenever she attempted to crawl through the door, her father would say that she was just impatient to ride her first horse. She picked up the sword before she could speak and the bow was not far behind, both of which she excelled at. When she did speak, her first words were a war cry she had learned from her father.

As is typical of Varza, she could sometimes be a cruel child. She learned the power of strength at a young age when she stole the toys of those smaller than her or bloodied those who called her names. But, as she grew to a wiser age, she learned the proper Koureki way, that the Varza should defend the weak, not prey on them. She imagined herself as Durukhi, slaying elephants and Gashgha, beheading the witches. It was not rare for her to bash sticks with another child, sometimes from horseback, other times atop the walls of Kourek. Her active, spirit thrilled her father. With four previous daughters, all of whom leaned toward the Shava path, he had nearly given up hope of fostering a Varza. He finally had the warrior he hoped would follow in his footsteps.

Sometimes her insistent begging wormed its way into his heart and he would let her play with his Varza mask, proof of his bravery and skill. She would run through the streets wearing the mask, its feathers bouncing from her play and her gleeful eyes peering wide behind the eye slits carved into the dark wood. Her father had to track her down and pry it from her reluctant fingers, but that only made him happier.

The purpose of a Varza, however, was not to wear masks. It was to defend the Koureki and drive their herds. A Varza's most important weapon, tool and ally in their duties was not their sword or bow. It was the bond that stitched together a horse and a Varza, and Edjeera longed for this bond.

When she had proven herself upon the ponies and elderly horses, her father introduced her to his herd, from which she might choose her favorite. Her eye was immediately drawn to the wild stallions that were quick to rear and quick to bite. She approached the boldest of these beasts, thinking her own boldness to be a match. But for all the wildness of her spirit, she was still but a little girl and she cowed away from the might of the stallion's flailing hooves.

So instead, her father brought forward a youthful, proud mare; one who would not give up easily but restrained from flailing her hooves so wantonly. Edjeera struggled with this creature the entire morning, urged on by the constant support of her father. But before the sun had reached its highest, Edjeera no longer stood before the horse but atop its back.

With a slap to the horse's rear, Edjeera's father sent the beast barreling forward with Edjeera screaming and clinging to the saddle. As the grassy hills passed beneath her, her screams turned to delighted squeals. On that day, she fell in love with the wind, with the plains and with her horse. When the beast had slowed down to a trot and was returning on its own to the rest of the herd, Edjeera began throwing out names to the creature, asking which one the mare liked most. When the horse sneezed, Edjeera interpreted that as approval and the beast was thereafter known as Geda.

It took her years to properly commune with Geda, to communicate her wishes to the horse through the subtle movement of her legs, hands and shifting weight. When Geda finally understood, they flew over the grassy hills with such speed and grace that Edjeera wept from joy. It was not long before she combined this joy with her skill with a bow and sword. She learned how to keep her balance when slashing from horseback and how to time her shot during a full gallop. She no longer considered a day finished until she had ridden upon the plains and returned with a dead burrowing rat, one of her arrows protruding from its side.

CHAPTER 3

Edjeera had more than just her father's fire and skill. She also boasted her mother's beauty. As she grew, she caught the eye of a proud, handsome youth named Jurkarthi. The lad was half as heavy as a horse and taller than a man's spear. He rode a horse with the skill of the nomads and he could hit a rabbit in the eye even under a heavy wind. He desired her, so he made his affection plain. When he rode in her company, he would drive his horse to outpace everyone else. When they played Bolaa, he would move like the wind itself, wrestling the sheep's head from his opponent's grasp and plowing past everyone who stood before him to the other team's post. Every time he did something he thought might impress her, he looked to her for a reaction.

But Edjeera had no eyes for Jurkarthi. If she paired with him, she could only ever be a Shava to his Varza. Instead, she found another, who befitted her better, who could fit his Shava with her Varza. She found him as she rode up to the Cave of the Gods, where the many spirits that watch over or impede us sit patiently on their pedestals. The day before, the rock around the cave's maw was grey and dull, but as she came upon it now, her mouth fell open in awe. The wall of stone was now ablaze with colors. Horses, wolves, rabbits and eagles—of reds, blues, browns and blacks—ran or flew against a changing background of yellows, whites, greens and oranges, a swirl of color that perplexed the mind, but dazzled the soul. Higher on the wall, white stars bathed light upon the simple creatures below as they paraded across the open plains and rolling hills of the steppe. Strange lines and spirals, and other shapes Edjeera had no name for, twisted among the creatures, all of them leading toward or facing a single spot where the rock was still bare.

There she saw him, sitting cross-legged before this blank spot. A mess of paints blotted his legs and arms. His tunic would require thorough washing. He stared at the spot, so lost in his thoughts that he did not hear her approach until she spoke.

"It's beautiful," Edjeera said, "but why have you done this?"

He did not seem surprised by her sudden appearance. Perhaps he had actually known she approached after all. Instead, he turned to look back at her before returning his gaze to the wall.

"Hmm?" was the sound he first made before words came to him, "I dreamt this last night and so I felt bade to paint it. It looked better in the dream."

"Did the gods send you this dream?" she asked. "They must have desired it."

"Yes, I think that is so. They seemed so lonely, sitting in a cold cave, with only the color of our meager offerings."

"But, will it not wash away in the next rain?"

"Hmm...," he said, pondering the issue. "I suppose you're right. I would need to start again, and paint something grander."

Edjeera's eyes drifted back toward the blank spot.

"Why have you left this part untouched?"

"I want to paint a person, to stand at the center of all this," he waved a hand, gesturing at his art. "But I do not think I can do it justice. Not from just my memory."

An idea came to Edjeera.

"I can be the person. Use me as your model and I will stand just so," she placed herself where the absent person would go and rested her hands on her hips, standing defiantly at the center of his universe.

The youth's eyes sparkled and he leapt to his feet. Edjeera now saw him fully, in his beautiful, lithe form. His paint-smeared lips curled into a smile and he broke into a laugh.

"A very good idea. Let me get my paints."

She knew he would be hers. Within three new moons, they announced their love and asked their families and the sages to join them. The sages asked the gods and the gods favored the match. Edjeera's own parents approved. The youth, Tanjiati, was to be a sage himself one day and Edjeera's marriage to him would bring the gods' favor upon her family. His father wanted him to be Varza, but his path to Shava had been plain to everyone else. Taking refuge in the knowledge that his other sons had already earned their Varza masks, he finally compromised with Tanjiati.

They built a home by the lakeside, where Tanjiati could siphon water to grow his vegetables. He would grow their food and continue his apprenticeship as a sage, while Edjeera rode her horse upon the steppes and hunted and herded. Every day, she would return, aching and sweaty, to find some new painted figure upon the hut's side, until the entire structure was a mural of beautiful overlapping animals and people. Whenever an old creation faded a new one took its place. The daily surprise delighted her.

Upon their bonding day, as the sun was failing in the west, turning the grass into a great expanse of orange and red, she took him riding.

Geda carried them both far until Edjeera slowed her to a halt upon the highest hill that overlooked Kourek. There, under a canopy of stars, they made love. Loyal Geda munched patiently upon the grasses nearby.

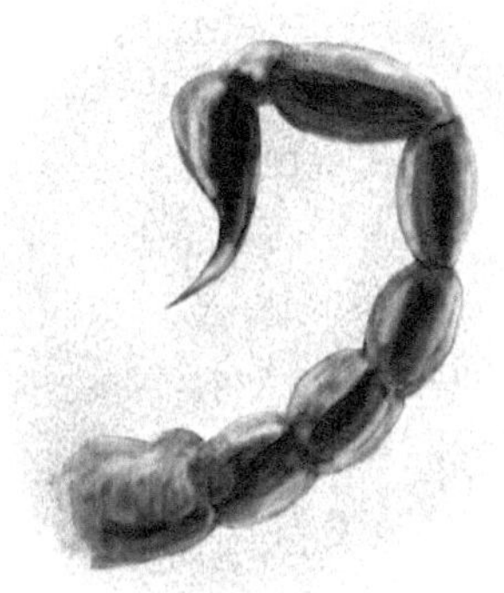

Chapter 4

The Koureki had always worked hard to keep the peace with the nomads who ruled the plain. Their hordes heralded from no cities, and theirs was a tough lot. Whereas the Koureki trained in the saddle from age seven, the nomads rode at three. They cultivated no fields, fished in no lakes, and lived under canvas, hide and sky rather than clay. They were a herding and hunting people, and they traded their goat dairy and yak fur for fresh fish, vegetables and pots. This trade worked for all and no one felt the loser. But, the nomads were an impatient, unbalanced people. Some Koureki liked to say it was because they had no home to come back to, and that led them to drift. Others said it is because they let one sex rule the other and in so doing, could not find the balance that the other sex provided. But, their reasons and minds were as alien as those of the buffalo, and if their whims told them to betray their relationships, they would do so.

Word spread throughout the city that a band of Tichnik bug-women were pillaging outlying farms of their crops, stealing away animals from the herdsmen, and even once cajoling their horses into swimming far enough to capture a Koureki fisherman who had strayed too close to the shallows. The fisherman, the herdsmen, and the farmers all came before the council of eleven, desiring retribution. So, the council dispatched fifty riders to apprehend or, if necessary, kill the Tichnik. It was decided that the group would be composed of the young warriors, who had yet to be tested in battle, so that when a true threat came upon the city, these warriors would already know the danger they would be facing. They would be led by the great hero Sandrial, who had once defended a watchtower by himself against fifty Refinn warriors.

Edjeera was chosen to go, but she was ready. This would be her rite of passage into a true Varza, which would earn her the first mask. The elders had seen her practice, and knew her skill with the bow and saddle. They knew she would be among the best. Her father gave her his sword. It was a slender, curved thing that he claimed could shear the head off a horse if the rider were galloping fast enough. She lifted it from his spread hands and waved it in graceful, deliberate arcs, testing its balance. It was a great honor to receive this sword, as well as a great responsibility. When she left his presence, she clutched it close to her chest as if fearful that a strong gust might carry it off.

As the sun rose on the morning of departure, Edjeera mounted her horse beside the other warriors who were arranged inside the city gates. Men, women and children gathered around the force of fifty Varza, giving them parting gifts, celebrating their glory, but also wishing them safe return. Tanjiati provided an ivory token of protection and dabbed her forehead with sweet-smelling oil for luck. Edjeera's mother wept openly and held the girl's hands firm in her grasp, demanding that Edjeera return home safely. Even her father shed one tear before wiping his eyes. To shed more than one tear as a Varza is disgraceful, something Edjeera would need to be heedful of after that day.

Edjeera maintained a posture of severity, but inside she felt unsteady, as if she stood on the tips of grass blades. The path of Varza had always called to her, but this would be the first time she put her bravery to the test. The Tichnik were notable among the Koureki for their fearful appearance. Edjeera had heard stories of the four-armed, armored creatures. She heard of their screaming hiss and their blood-colored eyes. But their most fearful aspect was their poisonous tail, for which there was no cure. Edjeera tried to not to let the stories shake her, but a root of fear had dug its way into her heart, one she hoped would not blossom during her great test.

The gates creaked open, and the hero Sandrial coaxed his mount forward. The other warriors commanded their steeds to follow. As she rode past, Edjeera met the eyes of first her mother, then her father, and finally her lover. His face, too, was damp with a sheen that caught the midday sun. He watched her but did not speak. He did not need to, for Edjeera knew he was wishing her a safe return.

The riders passed through the gates, and the urban clay-and-straw buildings were replaced by tents and crude canvas dwellings. Finally, they emerged onto grassy hills seemingly without end. Sandrial led them into a gallop and they stormed the plains with a thunderous rhythm that matched Edjeera's heartbeat. The wind thrashed at their faces, forcing them to squint, but Edjeera had never felt so free and alive, though anxiety still welled in her stomach.

To her dismay, however, Jurkarthi had also been chosen. He had been spiteful ever since learning of her chosen lover; he was not used to girls rebuking his advances and had begun striking back in many small ways. Once, he and his band of thugs had followed Tanjiati back from his watch at the temple. They never caused trouble, but watched him with stares that hinted at violence. His spiteful nature had led him to spin stories about her, saying that she never bathed, or liked snuggling with horses. Edjeera had tracked him down as the source of these awful lies, and had gathered Tanjiati's brothers and her own cousins to force him into silence. The lawkeepers had to settle the brawl she and Jurkarthi had started. Each received lashes for their unruliness, but still their feud persisted.

The sun was not three hands into the sky when Jurkarthi dropped back to ride beside Edjeera. Above the din of the hooves, he narrowed his eyes and shouted how frightened she looked. The observation stung, for though Edjeera rode stoic in the saddle, lizards scrambled in her stomach. She stung back, shouting "I'll spare you a tear when you return riding behind the honored dead."

The suggestion of his cowardice did not stop him. He taunted that she could hide behind him, that he would protect her from the savages. He yelled that it was not too late, that she could run back home and become his Shava. These words incensed Edjeera to challenge him, but Sandrial intervened, ordering that now was not the time for a challenge, that such a fight could happen after the Tichnik were dealt with.

As he said these words, one of the scouts rode up to Sandrial to report. The Tichnik had been sighted. With this exciting news, they drove their steeds into a gallop and raced over the flowing, grassy hills, hoping to catch the bug-women off guard. They needed to hurry, for though the Tichnik had been encamped, it was hard to stay hidden among the grasses. Edjeera's stomach grew heavier still, and her hands tightened around the reins.

As they crested a line of hills, they came upon a crater in which the Tichnik had made their camp. Here no grass grew, only the hardiest and shrewdest plants. It was a brown stain upon the pristine grassland. Edjeera knew of this place, though she had never visited it. Long ago, an army of invaders, marching row-upon-row and mounted upon elephants and rhinos, had sought to conquer Kourek. But, the Koure-ki warriors were too clever for them and had ensnared the invaders within this crater and enacted vengeance upon the creatures. Their bones still littered the bottom of the broad, barren depression.

Edjeera did not notice these bones, but instead she had eyes only for the smoke wafting from the Tichnik cooking pits and the tents scattered about those fires. The Koureki must have been spotted, for the bug-women were mounting their horses or attempting to pack their belongings and their loot.

Sandrial hollered his war cry and charged into the crater. The rest of the Koureki mimicked him. Any unmounted Tichnik hastily did so, leaving tents still standing and wrapped food only partially buried beside hot coals. The hooves of the Koureki mounts beat against the stony ground like a wave of thunder, a menacing presence that Edjeera did not feel in her heart as she clung to the reins of Geda.

As the Tichnik rode toward the edge of the crater, one of their horses collapsed and the rider was flung forward to sprawl in the dirt before her screaming mount. This happened several more times, although none of the Koureki had fired their arrows. The Tichnik horses had just collapsed from under their riders, splaying both.

"Burrowing rats!" Sandrial shouted as a warning. "We go around. Follow me!"

He led them to the right and Edjeera saw that once the Tichnik had passed, little rodents emerged from the ground and chittered angry chirps at the screaming, writhing Tichnik horses and their fallen riders. At Sandrial's command, two Koureki broke from the rest of the war-party and dismounted to deal with the fallen Tichnik, without stepping in the burrowing rats' holes.

Going around the rodent holes delayed the Koureki, giving the Tichnik enough time to climb the slope of the crater. As the Koureki ascended behind them, resuming their war cry, the Tichnik turned around and screamed their own hissing cries. It was as if a thousand rattlesnakes descended upon the Koureki. The bug-women's fanged mouths were open wide and their eyes were the color of blood. A tail curled up behind each of their heads, and at the tip a scimitar point stood poised. Each sported four arms, with two guiding their mounts and the other pair holding their bows. Arrows leapt from their hands to soar toward the Koureki.

The treacherous sky hid the missiles until it was too late, and Edjeera heard them hissing past her. She clutched more tightly to her mount. Sandrial called for the Koureki to fire back. Leading his horse with his feet, he held aloft his bow and produced his own arrow, which sprang from his tightened form. Edjeera urged herself to retrieve her own bow. She had fired from horseback many times against dummies or steppe deer. But her body disobeyed her, for she could not reach for her bow. Instead, she lay flat against Geda, as if raising her head above the horse's own would invite an arrow to pin her.

Beside her Jurkarthi saw this and laughed. He, too, was hunched, his own body betraying his courageous front, but he teased her nonetheless.

"Foolish girl! Run back now before your pretty face gets..."

He could not finish his sentence. An arrow punctured his collar. It slid through his flesh and emerged through his back, the missile's head black with his blood. Jurkarthi did not scream, but seemed surprised. He reached up to where the arrow was embedded, but lost his balance and fell from his horse. His foot caught in the saddle's stirrup and he was dragged with his face grinding through the coarse ground before his horse slowed enough that Edjeera lost sight of him.

The sight paralyzed her. The memory of his punctured body seared into her mind. The Tichnik unleashed another volley and two more riders were struck: one to Edjeera's left and another to her right. They both screamed and their faces contorted with agony. The cries awoke something inside Edjeera. She found she could move again, but instead of raising her sword above her head or firing her own arrow, she turned Geda around and fled back the way they had come.

Edjeera flew past Jurkarthi's horse and past the trail of deep red. She passed the burrowing rats, as her two Koureki companions cut the throats of the pleading, fallen Tichnik. She passed the abandoned camp and flew up the side of the crater from where they had descended, back into the grassy hills. The grass flowed below her as a great green blur. Tears cascaded from Edjeera's eyes and, powered by the wind, streaked across her cheeks. A little voice inside her screamed out and with feeble authority, ordered her to rejoin her fellow warriors. It was the duty she owed them. But fear was her driver now and she obeyed only its command.

Edjeera didn't know how long she had ridden, but when she finally came to a halt, she found herself atop the peak of a hill with nothing but the swaying grasses surrounding her. Her only companion was Geda, who breathed in gasps of air as froth dripped from her lips. Edjeera looked about, seeking out her fellow warriors. With the worst of her shock now tempered, she desperately considered rejoining them and restoring her honor. But they were far behind her. If they survived, the battle would likely be over.

Instead, she screamed to the empty hills. She screamed into the winds that danced about her like her roiling emotions.

CHAPTER 5

That was where the victorious hunters found her. They had caught and slain all the Tichnik bandits, ridding the Koureki countryside of their stain. Tichnik heads bounced against the sides of their mounts, tied by their antennae to the Koureki saddles; quivers bulged with new arrows and empty horses now carried the stolen wealth of the thieves. The Koureki were in good spirits and joked among themselves, but they ignored Edjeera. They reacted to her only when she attempted to join the column, sidling up next to her childhood friends. Edjeera tried to act as if she had done nothing dishonorable, but her former friends were disgusted.

"To the back of the line!" they said. "You do not deserve to ride with us."

With head bowed, she rode behind the corpses of those of her companions who had fallen. Jurkarthi lay on his belly in front of her, drooping over the sides of his horse. The felling arrow had been removed, but his face had been split open from being dragged behind his steed. She could hardly recognize him now. Yet, he was given a greater honor than she. Her gaze fell upon the other fallen warriors and each had suffered gaping, bloody wounds that were horrific to behold. Though the sight made her sick in her stomach, she could not look away and felt some relief that she had not suffered the same fate.

So engrossed in her thoughts was she that she hardly noticed Sandrial slip beside her. He watched her a moment before speaking.

"The Tichnik held the symbol of the hawk. They were of the Kehserris tribe. We will need to punish them to make them remember not to trouble the Koureki. It would be a good time to regain your honor."

Edjeera knew this should be welcome news. He was offering her redemption. But looking upon the mutilated body of Jurkarthi and the other slaughtered warriors, she remembered the panic that had stricken her. Her hands trembled, and her breathing hastened.

"Or..." Sandrial said, "there is also the path of the Shava."

With that, he left her to her fears.

The warriors returned home to great applause, though none was directed toward Edjeera. Her status in the column, behind the dead, was a clear sign of her dishonor. She searched the crowd for her father's face, but when she saw it, she regretted having looked. He was smiling when she first caught a glimpse of him, but when their eyes met, his glow faded and his face grew somber. Her gaze drifted to her mother, but she wouldn't even meet her daughter's eyes. She dreaded her coming confrontation with them.

When the procession was over, they met within the central room of their home. As she passed through the beaded entrance and let them clatter behind her, her parents rose from the cushions upon which they had been seated. Edjeera's sisters had been dismissed from the house. Her mother approached first.

"Well, you are unhurt," her mother told her bluntly, "that's good. Next time, you will do better."

Edjeera's father followed. He stopped short of her and inhaled. She braced for his anger, hoping she could hold firm. Instead, he stepped forward and embraced her. It was brief, but it was full of understanding. He knew the fears she faced upon the Varza path. When he stepped back, his face had turned to stone, with only slight tremors betraying his stoicism.

"She is right. There will be a raid against the Tichnik to show them the folly of challenging us. You will join it."

Edjeera could not match her father's gaze, so she looked down at her feet. She could feel her eyes growing wet. Jurkarthi's ruined face flashed across her mind. Straight-backed, her father waited for her answer.

"I cannot go on that raid," she said finally.

Her father did not shout or curse her, but the disappointment held taut in his face was far worse.

She could not stay in that house any longer. She fled and sought refuge with Tanjiati. He was patient with her and showed no disappointment. That was why she loved him. They cradled each other in their garden, looking out upon the lake as the sun turned its waters to a glistening orange. It was there that she revealed the fears that arose when she turned to flee, and that she could not stand against those fears if she faced battle again. She did not know how she would earn her Varza mask, and her voice croaked as she admitted it.

When he did not respond, she looked upon his face and saw his own fear and doubt. But, eventually, he nodded.

"You will find a way," he said with unconvincing certainty, "I suppose... if you wish to... I can be your Va..., your Varza."

Edjeera shook her head, but did not know how to answer. They merely sat in silence as the reddening sun sank toward the lake's lapping waters.

Chapter 6

In the following days, word of Edjeera's failure passed from mouth to mouth. Neighbors avoided eye contact or glared at her. Other Varza, even those she had befriended, refused to speak with her, except for a few who told her to abandon the Varza path. No one except for ignorant foreigners would buy the milk she harvested from her goats or the hair she shaved from her yaks.

But, not everyone despised Edjeera. One day, as she milked her goats, she looked up as a pack of young Varza hopefuls came by and asked if she might join them in a game of Bolaa. They needn't have asked her twice, and, not long after, she and Geda raced across the fields outside Kourek's walls, tossing the sheep's head to allies and intercepting it from foes. The young Varza laughed and sometimes fought and argued, but such conflict only heightened the competition and improved the game.

For a little while, she forgot her problems. It did not matter that she had run from the Tichnik. It did not matter that she was a pariah to all but her closest kin. All that mattered was the wind kissing her cheeks, the laughter of her young friends and the exhilaration of racing past enemy riders and reaching the post. Her fear and shame disappeared.

As Geda galloped across the field, an ally tossed the head her way. She saw it growing larger as it approached, until she swiped it from the air. But then she hesitated. Where the ball had been, there was now a figure, dark and shady against the bright green and blue of the land and sky. The figure was horse-bound and its cloak wafted in the wind like a dark, amorphous cloud. A hood stretched over its face where no light touched, despite the bright sun. Its horse was so black that it looked akin to a gaping hole in her vision. The rider did not gallop, but let its horse trot calmly forward, its own posture swaying, but confident. It was in no rush.

By now, her friends had seen the rider as well and they paused in their play to watch it approach. One boy called out, demanding that the figure name its tribe or city. The rider did not answer, and so the boy tried again. Edjeera and her friends shuffled on their mounts and their horses stomped with nervous giddiness.

When the rider refused to answer a second time, the boy took out a short sword and charged his mount toward the shadow figure. He waved the sword over his head, trying to intimidate the rider, but without success. The boy pulled up short and threatened to kill the rider if it did not name itself. So, when the rider did not, he charged again and swung at its neck.

Neither the rider nor its horse flinched. The boy's sword swung true but had no effect, and the figure rode on as if nothing had happened. The boy turned his mount around and swung at it three more times and twice at the horse. It was as if he slashed at air.

It was then that Edjeera realized with sickening dread that the rider walked toward her. She turned her mount around toward the city gate, gazing back to track the rider's path. Some of her friends did the same, unnerved by the creature.

As Edjeera moved toward the gates, the rider changed its direction to follow her. Edjeera felt the same fear that had welled inside her upon seeing Jurkarthi's death. She prodded her mount to walk faster and, looking over her shoulder, she saw the rider quickened as well. Her friends rode behind her, unnerved by the stranger's presence.

Edjeera looked back at the gates. Whereas she had previously wanted to play far from the city, its great distance horrified her now. She cajoled Geda into a tepid run. Looking around, she saw that the rider had done the same. Some of the other children had strayed out of its course, but the stranger did not notice them and maintained its direction toward Edjeera. Four children rode between them, casting nervous glances over their shoulders as well.

Edjeera spurred Geda into a full gallop, but the rider did the same. The children who still followed her sped up as well, but Geda was the fastest and outpaced them all. When she looked over her shoulder, the rider passed the first child, ignoring him. She looked back at the gate. It appeared the size of a bead. The rider passed the second child. The gate looked the size of a plum. She coaxed Geda to run faster, so much so that she was nearly blinded by the rushing wind. The rider passed the third child. The gate seemed the size of her palm. She placed aside the thought that if her friend's blade did little good against the rider, what hope could all the blades of Koureki have. She rode anyway. When she looked back again, the rider had eclipsed the fourth child and it was clear that she was its target. Then, it took out a long, curved sword.

She reached for an arrow from her sheath, but found none there. She had not planned on using them while at play. She demanded that her steed go faster. The hooves of Geda pounded the ground and shook her with each rhythmic thump. She felt like a speeding eagle, but the rider closed the distance without great effort.

As it drew closer, the stranger raised its sword above its head, causing its hood to slip back enough to reveal its face. What Edjeera saw could not be. It was only a glimpse, but she instantly recognized the bloody mess of flesh and gristle that had been Jurkarthi's face. She had seen his body placed inside the burial mound after they returned to the city. But here it was oozing blood, its nose shredded, its eyes hidden beneath swollen and torn bulges, and its rows of teeth curled into a perpetual grin.

Edjeera had never felt the need to scream before, even as she fled from the battlefield. It was never her way. But now she could not stop the sound from leaving her lips, and she wailed as she passed under the city gates. The rider stopped.

When Edjeera realized it was no longer upon her she slowed Geda to a stop and whirled around. At the open gates, the rider sat upon its motionless horse, watching her from beyond the arch. Its face was again hidden by shadow. Two archers who guarded the gate fired upon the rider, but their arrows slid through it and disappeared into the grassy steppe. Edjeera shivered and rode away.

Chapter 7

By the time the sun had departed in the west, the specter, now standing motionless outside the gates, was just a deep, malevolent shadow against the black grasses. But every Koureki had learned of Edjeera's spirit. When she passed in the streets, she drew their cautious gazes and when they thought she was out of earshot, she could hear their whispered gossip.

That night, a mob descended upon the council of sages and demanded an explanation of the mysterious rider and a solution on what could be done. Traders, peddlers, shepherds and slavers all feared for their safety should their business take them outside the city. For now, the rider ignored everyone except Edjeera, but for how long would that last?

The Koureki warriors feared that the steppe tribes or other plains cities might take the rider as a sign of Kourek's decay and seek to conquer the city to remove its blot from the land. They demanded that Edjeera be delivered to the rider, so that it might finish its purpose and leave the rest of the people alone.

But Edjeera did not pay these matters any mind. She chose instead to speak with Tanjiati. He had studied much in the way of the sage, and she trusted him to know how she might be rid of it. He listened to her entire story, never speaking a word until she was finished. Then, he left that very night for the cave of the gods, where he communed with them until the sun rose again. That night had been her longest, for she had neither family nor spouse to comfort her. She had been left alone in the dark hut, praying that the rider did not find her there. So, when Tanjiati came back, she scrambled to embrace him, before falling to her knees and asking what she might do.

"You say that mortal weapons had no effect on him," he repeated and Edjeera nodded. "Then it is likely a spirit, a creature that can project onto our world but can do little else. It was likely sent after your retreat from..."

He paused, but Edjeera understood what he meant.

"It was sent to punish me," she continued, "for my failure."

"No, not to punish, but to teach. Perhaps just as nothing can harm it, it can harm nothing. The spirit is here to teach you to become brave."

Tanjiati gave her a rattle, dabs of a sweet-smelling oil and a small censer with incense. He taught her two recitations; one to banish the spirit and the other to call a greater spirit or god to pull the spirit back to its realm. When she had memorized the chants, she clad herself in her old Varza armor and buckled her sword. She did not know if they would help, but she felt a little more secure wearing such protections. Tanjiati applied paints to her face and tied her hair in braids like those of the greatest warrior gods. When Edjeera mounted Geda, she leaned over to the horse's ear and told her to be brave, even as she fought to be now. Geda twitched her ear and stomped.

With Tanjiati walking next to her, Edjeera rode to the gate where the rider still waited. When she saw it, sitting atop its steed of shadow, her hands trembled. She fought the urge to turn around, to resolve never to leave the city again. She reached a hand down to Tanjiati and he squeezed it.

"It's only a test," he said, "do not be fooled by it."

She nodded and coaxed her mount through the gate. The rider watched her from atop its horse an arrow's flight away. Neither horse nor rider moved. Edjeera felt the urge to drop the censer and rattle and draw her sword, but she fought that instinct. Behind her, a small crowd clustered at the gates, but no one spoke above a whisper. The only sounds were the wind gently caressing the grass stalks, and the dry dirt cracking under her horse's hooves.

She began reciting both chants, one after the other, while shaking the rattle with intensifying vigor and bathing herself in smoke. She fought the urge to cough and interrupt her rhythm. The spirit did not run away or disappear, however. It waited for her approach.

After she had recited both chants three times, the rider finally moved. It took out its bow. Edjeera swallowed and remembered that Tanjiati had said the spirit couldn't hurt her. The rider pulled an arrow from its quiver. It was a test, Edjeera repeated to herself, so that she might prove her bravery. She shunned any other doubting thought. The rider nocked the arrow, stretched it back and aimed it at the girl. It was a cool day, yet still her palms sweated and trembled. But she did not turn back.

Then, the arrow flew. She flinched, but it struck her below her right breast, slamming into her with the strength of a punch not even the strongest man could match. She looked at it in horror as it protruded through her armor into her flesh below. But, she felt nothing. She was on the cusp of rejoicing when pain exploded from the wound. The rattle clattered to the ground, followed by the censer. She screamed and nearly fell off her horse as Geda panicked, bolting unbidden toward the city gates.

Blood flowed along the shaft, but she pulled her gaze away to seek the rider. It was already bearing down on her, with sword leveled to take off her head. She knew not where the strength came from, but she managed to pull her own sword free and raised it to take the brunt of the incoming blow. The rider's sword slammed into hers and knocked it from her hand, but her parry had done enough. The blow cut into her shoulder pad, but did not reach flesh.

The rider raised its sword for another strike, but the shadow horse slowed to a halt just as Edjeera crossed through the gate's threshold. She felt no relief, however, as every move she made hurt. She suddenly felt faint and looked up to see Tanjiati running up to her.

He took Geda's reins so that Edjeera could be dismounted and carried to the temple of the sages. They used their strongest rituals and recited their strongest chants, and applied their best herbs to the wound and down Edjeera's throat. But, the girl had lost much blood. A curious crowd gathered at the temple entryway after following the red trail Edjeera had left. She lost consciousness and Tanjiati wept that her life was failing. Edjeera's sisters, who had watched the entire encounter, fetched their mother and father, and each arrived at her side to pray for her recovery. Edjeera's father shed his one tear, whispered a little prayer and left to ride among the hills, alone except for his thoughts. Outside the city, the spirit merely waited. As night fell, the sages predicted, with downturned faces, that, despite their best efforts, the girl would not last the night.

But they were wrong. Edjeera's wound healed with remarkable rapidity, and when the sun rose the next day, the wound bled no longer. She awoke from her stupor, aching all over her body, as if the sages, instead of healing her, had pounded her head with a mallet the entire night. Her stirring surprised and delighted Tanjiati, who had sat by her side the entire night, keeping her own hand in his. His first words were a tearful apology as he clutched her hand. It was his advice that had led to her suffering and close demise.

Among the sages was Urdanti, the wisest of them all. She overheard Tanjiati's rambling and was astonished to find Edjeera propping herself up in bed, even as she clutched at her forehead. Urdanti's astonishment grew still when she saw the condition of the wound. But her surprise did not last long, for she knew the history of her people well. This was not the first time gods and spirits had intervened in the lives of the Koureki.

She explained to Edjeera, that the rider was a test meant only for her, since only she could apparently interact with it. But it was not a test that could be surpassed without loss. The rider, or the god who had sent it, did not want Edjeera dead, as proven by Edjeera's rapid recovery. However, Edjeera had to suffer if she desired to pass it. She would have suffered through her first test, the battle, if she had stayed. If she wished to become Varza, she would need to suffer through this one as well.

Hearing this, the sight of Jurkarthi's shredded face flashed through Edjeera's mind, searing like a bolt of lightning and followed by the lingering thunder of the pain in her side. She cried out that she no longer desired to be Varza.

"I will take the path of the Shava," she shouted, "the path of the Varza is one I can no longer stomach."

The wisest sage sought to protest, for she knew the path of the Shava was no easier, but Tanjiati, stirred by his partner's fear, spoke forth that he would take the path of Varza in her stead.

"When the next band of warriors rides out, I will go with them. If it will spare Edjeera greater pain," he said.

The sage hesitated a moment, finding the words she hoped would be the right ones.

"The choice is, in the end, yours," she said to them both. "But I see great hardship for you both, though you might be blind to it now."

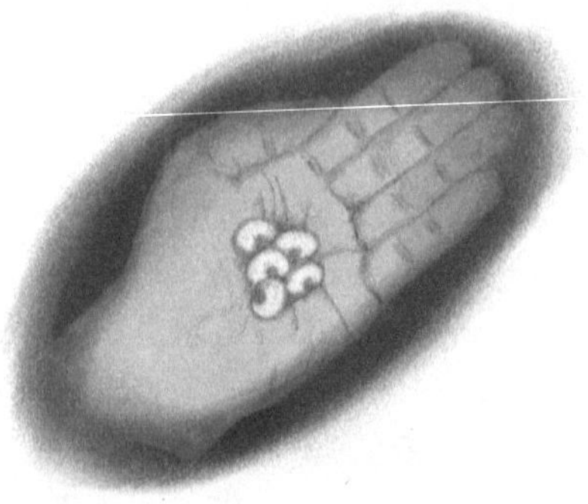

Chapter 8

That very same morning, Edjeera and Tanjiati approached the sages to ask the gods if they could change their paths. Edjeera beseeched them first. When she was finished, Tanjiati's request would follow. The sages retreated to their forbidden chambers and conducted their arcane rituals, asking the gods permission to change her path this late in her growth. Edjeera quaked with a great weight in her stomach, fearing either answer. She didn't want to face the horror of Varza nor the shame of Shava. When the sages returned, she was not surprised by the answer. Perhaps, because of her cowardice, the gods now accepted her path as Shava.

"However," Urdanti said, "a rite must be performed to change one's path." She gazed into the younger girl's eyes, "Young Edjeera, has Tanjiati ever told you how we discover the gods' will? How we know what is best for our people, by communing with the spirits?"

"He says you gather into a single hall and all together fall into trances. And once you finish, you have learned the gods' will."

"Yes, but in order to commune with the spirits, we must drink special remedies made from rare plants. Those seeking the Shava mask after walking the path of Varza must harvest the buds from those plants. But, they only grow in one place. A sacred place."

Edjeera's heart fell as she sensed what Urdanti's next words would be.

"A place outside of these walls," Urdanti finished. "You would need to leave this city to fetch those plants and bring them back to us. It is not a long journey, usually only five days at most. The grove is still within our territory and caravans travel much farther. But..."

"I will still have to face the rider," Edjeera's shoulders fell.

"There is another way," Urdanti said, "we keep a handful of seeds in Kourek. The gods have instructed us to offer them to you, and if you can care for and turn these seeds into leaves and buds, you will have proven yourself worthy of the mask of Shava."

The task seemed so simple that Edjeera agreed to it in a heartbeat.

She still needed her parents' consent, so Urdanti sent for them. Her mother arrived first and denied permission. She had known her vigorous daughter all of Edjeera's life. Edjeera was the daughter who turned her broom into a spear when she should have been sweeping or coated her body in flour when she should have been baking. Edjeera had not the natural temperament for Shava duties. Her mother would not let her so carelessly change her life. Only once Urdanti told her of the gods' decision did her rigidity break. She had not the conviction to condone the decision, but she would defer to the judgment of Edjeera's father. Since he shared the same path as his daughter, he would have the final say.

Her father arrived at the temple carrying Edjeera's fallen sword, the same he had long ago given her. He offered it back to her, but Edjeera avoided his eyes and shook her head. That was when he learned. She expected him to bluster and rage, but instead, his face twisted in poorly concealed disappointment. He knelt to see her wound and took her hand in his. Her father said nothing throughout the encounter, and when he finally left, he carried the sword with him. Again, he rode out onto the plains to be with his thoughts. When he returned at sundown, casting a vicious glare at the rider along the way, he came back to Edjeera's bedside, deflated and defeated. Her father sat beside her long enough that Edjeera feared the sun would burn out before he again spoke. But when she opened her mouth to speak, he looked at her wound and in a low, nearly inaudible voice, gave his acceptance of her choice.

Edjeera had never imagined she might pursue the path of the Shava, and so she had much to learn before she could earn the mask. Tanjiati taught her about tending to their garden crops, weaving their clothes, foraging for shellfish and crabs that lived along the lakeshore, caring for the chickens, sweeping the floor, and mending the roof and walls of their house. Edjeera had performed many of these tasks before, but that was when she was but a little girl, when choosing between Varza and Shava was a distant concern, much like her own death. The familiar actions reawakened memories inside of her and, as she surrendered herself to these tasks, the boredom she felt as a girl came flooding back.

She was especially concerned with the care of a future child. Had she followed the Varza path, she would have still needed to birth their child, since the gods in their capricious wisdom had not provided Tanjiati with the means, but the rest of the child's needs–feeding it, cleaning it, watching its every movement–would have been the responsibility of her mate, aided by a rented slave girl or a Shava-in-training. She remembered watching her own mother struggle with the care of her sisters while her father cared for the horses. The choice had been obvious to Edjeera.

The realization that this was the path she would lead–to find herself constrained to the home, to forego the way of the rider, and the arrow, and the open, wild hills–was cause for great weeping when she was alone. It may have only been because of Tanjiati's exhaustion, after a full day's training as a warrior and herder, that he never noticed her puffed, red eyes when he came back home as the sun glowed orange.

But these tasks were all that stood between her and the spirit, and so she put her focus and effort into completing them. She planted the seeds the sages had given her, placing them at the instructed depth and ensuring that the ground was moist. Every morning, as the sun peeked over the lake, she checked to see if the green tendrils poked through, and every morning she was disappointed.

All the while, the spirit maintained its vigil outside the gate.

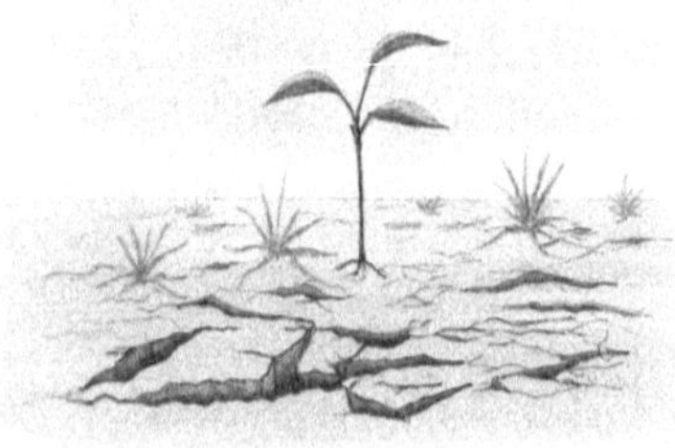

CHAPTER 9

The day came when Tanjiati was called forth to defend his city. A band of Tichnik vowed revenge over the execution of their brethren during Sandrial's retributive raid. News came from crying refugees that one of Kourek's client villages was now a smoldering ruin. The elders decided that these raiders had not learned the lesson that had been smote upon their dead brethren. A call for many warriors rang through the city and the sages compiled their list of the chosen. Tanjiati was named as one to prove himself.

From the time he learned of this to the moment he rode out the city gates, he uttered only a few words.

"I do this for you," he said on the day of his departure, smiling sadly as she examined his sword, ensuring the blade did not wobble in the handle. She had been providing him advice the entire morning, checking his tools, weapons and horse for signs of imperfection.

Now, he sat on his mount, Edjeera beside him on the ground and the dozen riders surrounding them, each saying their farewells. She looked up at Tanjiati's face and offered up his sword to him. So absorbed in his thoughts was he that it took him three times longer to tie his sword than it should have. He had been like this all morning and had spoken little.

"Come back to me," Edjeera said.

After seven days, he did, though not in the manner she expected. Embedded in the waiting crowd, she sought him out. The host's vanguard passed through, greeted with great cheer. Tanjiati wasn't among them, but that position was reserved for those who had acted with great valor. Neither was he among the other riders who preceded the dead. In horror, she scanned the bodies of the fallen. Jurkarthi's faceless mess returned to her mind, and she feared she would not even recognize her fallen lover. Finally, she saw him, sitting upon his tired horse, head bowed in shame, behind the bodies of the dead.

That night, they sat together inside their small hovel, faces flickering from the oil lamp. She had tried to support him as best she could. She had unburdened him of his armor and traveling clothes, settled him in their bed and prepared a basic dinner. She tried to act as if nothing had happened and treated him to the small news of their neighbors' doings. But, with the coming dark, his own silence finally pierced her, and she could find nothing left to say.

"Three days from now, a Borofid caravan leaves from the city to their homelands," he finally said. "They've requested Varza to guard them in their passage. I'll leave with them and hopefully I'll earn my mask."

He paused a moment, and Edjeera considered what he'd said.

"It seems a safer path to Varza," he continued. "I'll learn to barter. I'll learn where the wealthiest peoples are. I can make great riches as a trader's bodyguard, and support us that way."

After three days, he left again and, again, she was alone with her sweeping, gardening, weaving, and boredom. She repaired the holes in the roofing and walls of their hut, scoured weeds from her yard, and sewed patches over the holes in her garments. But each of these tasks took her days to complete. Often, Edjeera would find herself pausing and looking out over the lake at the fishermen. She wished she had been born a fisher's daughter so she might have earned her role of Varza on the lake.

Only in chasing the chickens did Edjeera find sport. When the time came to butcher one, she did not find the slowest bird and capture it. She stepped a few paces toward the flock, knife in hand, and when they shrank back–their caution not yet turned to terror–she felt a thrill shiver up her back. She stalked the flock, soaking in their uncertainty. Then, stepping lithely, she pounced forward, but not with her swiftest charge. She let them scatter in a dozen different directions. Even after choosing a target, she did not pursue it with determination. She would be arbitrary in her choice, and if another bird ventured too close, she chose that chicken as her prey instead. She did this several times. Whenever she neared the bird, it would panic and fly to the tallest building. She knew how to strike quickly to grab the bird before it flew, but she let her prey elude her, for otherwise that would be the end of her game.

But the game did end when a derisive voice called her and she turned to see her neighbor, a chicken hanging by its feet from her grip. The woman had already broken its neck, and it swayed, beak aimed toward the ground.

"Having trouble?" the woman asked. "Perhaps you need lessons."

Seething, Edjeera walked over, snatched the hen from her neighbor and stomped off.

Edjeera earned a reputation among her neighbors as sloppy and lazy. Holes would emerge in her home's roofing that should have taken under a day's labor to repair. But hers remained for many days because she ignored the problem until the rains prevented her from ignoring it any longer. Her garden was a scrappy patch where only the hardiest plants survived. Sometimes she even forgot to check on the sages' seeds, which needed much nourishment in that dry season. Only one sprout poked forth—one sprout between her and the rider.

Edjeera itched to take Geda into the hills, to outrace the wind and lie alone under a blanket of stars. She longed to chase the goats and oxen, to work with the dogs to keep the herds in line. She could do none of this while the rider waited outside.

Many suns passed overhead and one season changed to the next. Sometimes Edjeera would venture upon the city walls and watch the spirit ride in its long semi-circles back and forth. When it realized that she was watching, the rider would turn its abyssal face toward her and match her stare. Sometimes she would just watch it, with anger, fear and self-loathing storming amid her thoughts. Sometimes she would bring a cache of stones and throw them at the shadow, tying a bit of her fury to each one. The spirit would often stop its horse and watch as each stone uselessly thumped to the ground, far short of its mark.

One night, she ventured up with a quiver of arrows and a bow. She knew the rider was out of range as soon as she spotted its dark blotch. But she fired anyway, urging each arrow farther by her own frustrated will. As usual, the spirit stopped and stared at her pitiful attempts, and when she had lost her last arrow, she matched its gaze. They stared at each other longer than Edjeera could guess, before she noticed a string of torchlight slithering over the hills toward the city.

From the city's gate, a mournful horn wailed in the night, and a horn from the approaching riders answered. They were more Koureki, perhaps ten riders Edjeera judged by the number of lights. Her heart ached as she watched them, wishing she could be among their number.

These thoughts were dashed from her mind when another horn sounded, a higher-pitched one that screamed across the silent hills. There were dead or wounded riders among the group and the sages at the temple would need to be prepared to receive them. Edjeera's mind went to Tanjiati.

She reached the temple at the same time as the riders, and with horror discovered that her fears were not unfounded. She found him lying within, the wisest sage attending to his wound, applying her herbs, ointments and draughts. Edjeera scrambled to his side and grasped his limp hand. His entire left side was coated in blood, some dried, some fresh. Edjeera couldn't find the wounds until the sage pointed them out to her. There were three: two in his arm and a third in his side. As she worked, the sage explained how an arrow had pierced his left arm, gone through the other side and struck him in his rib. Tanjiati was lucid, but he was also unfocused; in order to dull the pain, the other warriors had gotten him drunk.

"I am here," she said, "I am here."

He did not speak, but he did meet her eyes and nodded. He winced at every shallow in-breath. Sweat thickly coated his brow. Yet, despite his suffering, he gave her a wide smile.

"I am alright. I am Varza now," he said.

"He's right," a voice said from behind her. It was Sandrial. "As he faced down one foe, a coward rode to his side and shot him. I saw it myself."

Sandrial looked toward Tanjiati and nodded, his expression somber.

"He still needs the ceremony, but I will stand as witness to his courage and his wound is proof enough. He has not received the piercing, but he is as good as Varza now."

"Only if he survives," Edjeera said, and then turned back to Tanjiati. "Do not die now, you hear? Do not!"

Chapter 10

Tanjiati obeyed Edjeera's command, and, though he did not recover from his wound as quickly as she had, his bleeding was contained to his bandages. He spent the next five days lying in the temple. His wound was dressed regularly by one of the sages, and each time a little less blood had soaked the cloth. Edjeera returned to him as often as possible and let their home deteriorate. One of her sisters noticed the decline and sent her daughter to tidy the house in Edjeera's absence.

Yet, despite Tanjiati's recovery, he did not rejoice. He talked little and what he did say was brief and without substance. Sometimes he might idly draw patterns into the floor with a piece of charcoal; the imagery took no recognizable form, yet something about the harsh, black shapes upon the gray flint tiles haunted Edjeera. She noticed how he stared unseeing, his mind lost in a shadowy gloom. But despite her queries, he would not share his deeper thoughts.

Every night, he suffered from nightmares. He called out in terror, cried in his sleep and begged for help, pleading sometimes to his mother, sometimes to his gods, and sometimes for Edjeera. When his tumult reached too great a climax, Edjeera would clutch at his slippery hand and whisper to him that he had nothing to fear, that she was here to protect him. He would never speak of the monsters that lurked in whatever land he dreamt, nor would he ever mention the terror he suffered.

Once, his cries awoke Urdanti. Edjeera heard her before she arrived in the room, the signature clop, clop, clop of her staff and the soft patting of her naked feet upon the carpet-dressed stone floor. Urdanti saw Edjeera leaning over Tanjiati's shaking form, moonlight shimmering off their dark faces.

Urdanti plodded toward Tanjiati and sat so that his head was cradled in her lap. She stroked his sodden forehead and whispered a soft lullaby in his ear until his trembling ceased and his cries turned to moans, and then to gentle breathing.

"I seek to relieve him of his pain, but I know not how you do it so effortlessly," Edjeera whispered, shaking her head.

"It is something you learn as Shava," said Urdanti, "in time, if you pay attention, you will learn as well."

Urdanti looked up at Edjeera.

"If Shava you still wish to be," she said.

"I cannot be Varza," Edjeera said, "I cannot face the creature outside. I cannot face a charging arrow. I cannot face... this." She motioned to Tanjiati.

"You are stronger than you think, Edjeera," Urdanti said, "and you will need to be, no matter which path you tread."

"There's no challenge in gardening or nurturing," Edjeera said, "Just boredom."

"Is that not a challenge in itself? To awaken, day after day, to the same chores, to the same work, to the same tasks that allow us and the Varza to survive? The Varza protect Kourek, but the Shava give it reason to exist. But the path of the Shava is not merely one of work. Learning patience, duty, and servitude are important, but also honing your wits and resilience. Unlike the Varza, the Shava does not look for trouble, but trouble will come to the Shava just the same. The Shava will need the greatest courage and wisdom to survive it. But you are not a survivor. You are a fighter."

She paused.

"I visited your home today," she continued. "I saw that one of your seeds sprouted. It doesn't seem to have survived. Your niece claims it was like that when she arrived."

A pit opened inside Edjeera, and she felt that at any moment she might fall in. The room suddenly seemed to tighten around her, choking off any escape. She was in the middle of the city, far from the spirit, yet she felt trapped. Despair climbed over her until the warm touch of Urdanti's hand covered Edjeera's own.

"If you must face it no matter the path, would you prefer to face it as a warrior or as a survivor? Would you prefer to live a life of quietude and work or one of excitement, but also danger? I have done both in my time, for both paths are important. But I cannot help but wonder if you stay by his side as much to avoid your duties at home as to look after him."

A fire stirred in Edjeera, and she wished to argue. But she knew in her heart that what Urdanti said was true.

"Do what you want to do," Urdanti continued, "Choose the path you want to follow. Shava or Varza, it does not matter. But, don't let that thing choose for you," she pointed toward the entrance to the temple, but Edjeera knew of what she spoke.

In time, Tanjiati's body recovered, but not his soul. He spoke not a word as Edjeera aided him back to their home and helped him into his bed. Her niece had done what repairs she could and fixed the holes in the hut and roof, but bristling weeds had invaded the garden. Edjeera knew something was wrong when Tanjiati took no notice of the ravagers that wrecked his beloved crops and instead passed without protest from the warm sunlight into the dim hut.

As he recovered, he would spend much of his time leaning against the mud wall of the hut, staring at the opposite wall or standing upon the lake's edge and watching its waves licking the beach, reaching out to his toes, but never quite mustering the strength to touch them. Tanjiati's paintings were worn and faded from his absence, but he made no effort to restore them, though Edjeera set bowls of paints beside him. He smiled, but only in a hollow way, a false grin that disappeared as soon as he thought no one was looking. The arrow might have well pierced his heart.

"Why do you brood so?" she asked him, "you are Varza, you have passed your test. You've proved that you are a brave, strong Varza."

"Yes, I am Varza now. Whenever we need warriors, I will be called upon. Whenever we face the dark, barbed arrows of the Refinn, I will be called upon. Whenever we must fight the carnivorous, monster bug-women, I will be called upon. Whenever Koureki must shed their blood and sacrifice their lives, I will be called upon. That arrow may have been removed, but I shall always carry it inside of me."

Edjeera saw Jurkarthi's mangled face and understood.

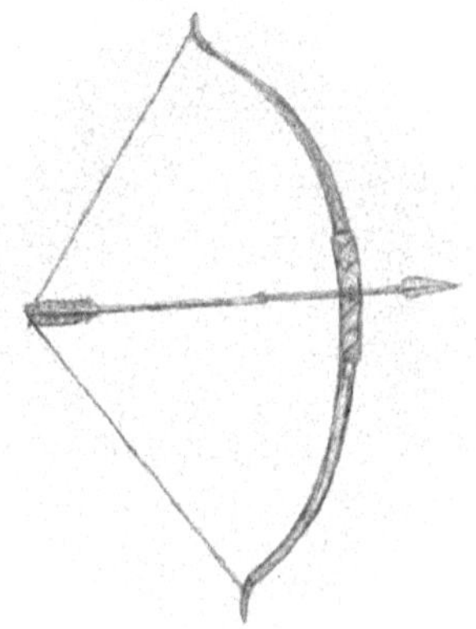

Chapter 11

Since Edjeera had failed to grow the sprouts, her first trial was arranged. She could no longer hide behind the walls of Kourek. She would need to earn her first Shava mask and undergo the first Shava piercings. She met in the temple at sunrise, where the sages dressed her in ceremonial garb, recited their chants and dabbed her in perfumes, oils and paints. They gave her a pack of supplies she would need for her journey: food, water, and a grinder and snipping tools so that she might prepare the flowers.

She then stepped toward the gate, each step tentative and uncertain, as if her destination would be her death. The sages trailed behind her, some armed with dried reed and seed rattles that hissed like a hundred snakes, and others beating two metal rods to a slow rhythm, with each strike shaking Edjeera to her bones. The rest of the sages chanted their protective spells, a dozen voices building in volume. A procession gathered around her, as the Koureki often did during such rituals. Some bystanders joined in the chanting.

When they arrived at the city gates, the procession ceased and the chanters turned to wailing as the doors were drawn open. The rattles hissed like a thousand vengeful vipers and the rods beat as if an army of iron horses stomped around her. When the doors could open no wider, the procession ceased its wailing and there was only silence. There was the rider, standing directly in front of the gate and to the side so that it did not impede her path. The spirit was dismounted and its weapons lay scattered in the dust around its feet. It reached out a hand and offered it to her. Edjeera raised her foot to step through the gate, but hesitated.

She feared what the spirit might do to her. It had dropped its weapons, but would it pick them back up as soon as she stepped through the gate? With her so defenseless, it could do any ghastly deed it desired.

But, she thought also of Tanjiati, and how he was willing to stubbornly, even perhaps unwisely, sacrifice himself for her comfort, comfort she did not truly desire. She remembered how he laid in tortured sleep, moaning from the wound in his side, a wound he took, walking a path he did not want. She recalled how vacant he seemed now, how he would stare without purpose, and how he stirred in his sleep.

Then, she thought of herself. She remembered the girl she once was, who held no fears and raced through the verdant hills with the wind splashing in her face. Her heart ached to do that yet again. She was brave once, before she understood the true consequences of the Varza path. Could she still be so brave now with that knowledge?

Edjeera placed her foot back down and reached her hand up to her face and hair to brush off the paints and ornaments. The crowd fidgeted and whispered around her like a sea of grass-blades brushing against each other.

"Fetch me my sword, my bow and Geda," she said.

At her words, the rider bounded toward its horse and leapt atop its back. Its bow, quiver and sword were reattached, but Edjeera never saw the spirit bend to pick them up. The rider gave one last look and coaxed its mount into a trot.

Behind her, the surprised crowd broke into a bustle of gossip. Urdanti's voice broke over the noise.

"You heard the girl! Someone bring her weapons and armor!" she ordered.

Several people scurried to obey the sage. Other Koureki shuffled in equal parts confusion and interest. But among the sages and her close family, there seemed to be a quiet understanding of her decision. Finally, her father appeared with her horse and weapons. He tried to remain stoic as he handed over each weapon, but she saw through his mask, which cracked at the corners of his mouth and in the twinkle of his eyes. She strapped her bow and quiver to her hip, slipped on her thumb-ring and ran her hands along her father's sword before attaching it to her hip; the movements were familiar and right as if meeting a long lost friend. Her father nodded to her, and she nodded back, feeling her rekindled passion flooding over her uncertainty like waves over dying embers. Whatever happened on those wide plains, she would bring her family the honor she had earlier forfeited.

Edjeera looked out through the gate once more and saw that the spirit was now a black blotch against the green hills, waiting for her approach. She then turned to Geda and stroked her soft fur. Edjeera hoped that fur would not be blemished by either of their blood by the day's end. She whispered in her mount's ear, "This is your test as much as mine. Give me your strength and speed, and I will ensure we both live through this day."

Her mount lowered her head into Edjeera's hands and the girl stroked Geda's mane. She climbed onto the horse's back. Pausing one last time before the gates, Edjeera searched the crowd for Tanjiati. But he was already by her side. He beckoned that she bend forward so he might whisper to her, and when she had, he spoke a soft "Come back to me."

"Always," she said and kissed him, before coaxing her mount forward and becoming one with the wind.

Chapter 12

The freedom of the hills expanded around Edjeera as she rode farther from the city, a grand openness that filled her. She couldn't help but unleash an echoing war-cry. She wailed and barked at the spirit, challenging it to face her, even as she reached for and felt the soft fletching of her chosen arrow.

But her opponent did not charge forward. Instead, the spirit retreated deeper into the hills. When Edjeera noticed this, she slowed Geda's gallop. If this was all she needed to do to pass this test, it seemed she had nothing to fear. However, her chest was still bruised and scarred from where the rider's arrow had struck her and she remained suspicious. As she slowed, the spirit whirled about and fired a lazy arrow in an arc toward her. With the wind beating at her eyes and the sun rising to her left, she lost sight of the dart as it merged with the sky. Edjeera estimated where the arrow would land and, with the image of Jurkarthi's ruined face still lodged in her mind, changed course to give the area a wide berth. Geda sped back into a gallop and the rider whirled around again and fled.

Again, Edjeera slowed Geda, and again the spirit turned and fired another arrow. She charged and the spirit fled. She understood now the game it played. It was trying to lure her deeper into the hills.

She considered turning back to Kourek since this seemed too obvious a trap. Goad your opponent into following you and then ambush them. If this were the case, no one could fault her for turning back. Her test couldn't mean she'd have to face an entire horde of spirits on her own. But she knew deep inside that if she turned around now, she would fail her test. If she were to be Varza, she must pursue and defeat the creature. So, she pressed Geda into a soft gallop, not wanting to tire her mount before confronting the spirit.

By the time the sun had reached two hand widths into the sky, the city was lost from view and she was alone in the hills, except for her stead and the rider, who kept just outside her arrow's reach. The spirit peppered her sporadically with arrows, ensuring that she would follow it and keeping her alert. She wondered how many arrows the rider kept in its quiver, and hoped it would keep wasting its precious stock, though the voice inside her knew such an outcome was unlikely.

Edjeera did not follow the rider in a straight line, instead seeking to maintain higher ground, so that she might better see if it truly was luring her into an ambush. She tried to maintain the same elevation as best she could, so that Geda would not tire from the sudden rises and descents. She followed lines of hills that led her in a different direction than the spirit, which seemed to irritate or worry the rider, as it would fire extra arrows at her. But Edjeera would always bend back toward the rider when the hills allowed and the spirit fled again.

As the sun rose to its peak, Edjeera understood now where the spirit was leading her, and she felt as if a batch of writhing snakes had slithered into her belly. She recognized familiar rocks and hill formations, and occasional copses of bushes and trees that she had not long ago passed. She came upon the hilltop where Sandrial and the other victorious riders had met her after she had fled. She paused only briefly at this spot, remembering her horror and shame when last she and Geda had stood there. The spirit was leading her back to the crater, where this whole nightmare began.

She looked at the rider, shielding her gaze from the sun. It still kept its distance, just outside of her arrow's reach, but this time it merely waited and did not press her to follow.

"I'm coming for you," she said. Though the spirit could not have heard her at that distance, it coaxed its horse into a trot in the direction of the crater. She watched it for a brief moment before telling Geda to follow.

Geda had tired from the chase and Edjeera chose to dismount and let her walk the rest of the distance. The spirit did not pressure her to follow at a greater speed. They had reached an understanding.

The sun had not yet set by the time she reached the crater's edge, but the grass glowed orange like stalks of wheat. A mist flowed like a pool of water within the crater's depths, shielding whatever lay below. It could not be an ordinary fog, for no mist lingered in the hills at this hour and it writhed like a fiercely blowing storm.

Within that smothering cloud, the spirit would have little trouble ambushing her. If she wasn't careful, it could dispatch her before she even realized it was upon her. Jurkarthi's image again flashed across her mind. On the way, Edjeera had imagined a thousand ways she might die, each more grotesque than the last. By the time she had actually arrived at the crater, her body trembled despite the warm air.

Edjeera's head turned back to the north, where her city dwelt unseen. She remembered her promise to Tanjiati. She would return. But she would bring back that creature's head with her.

"Geda," Edjeera said to her mount, "I really hate this creature. It doesn't fight fair."

Geda snorted and Edjeera mounted her. At Edjeera's request, Geda treaded forward, careful not to slip on loose rocks.

"I am by your side, Geda," Edjeera whispered into her mount's ear. "Guide me well. We can do this."

With these final words, they plunged into the writhing mists.

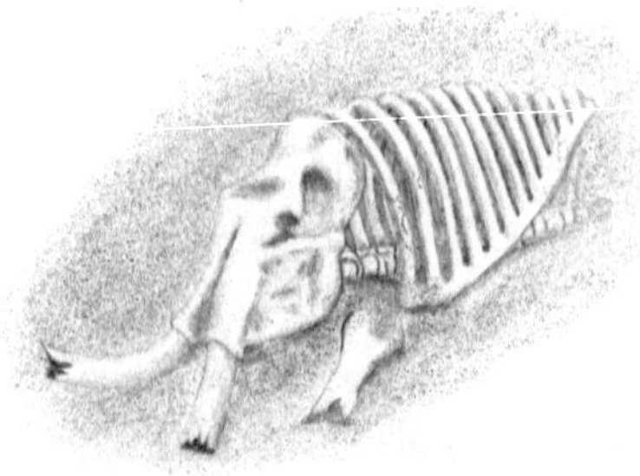

CHAPTER 13

The day had been a warm one, but in the mist-laden crater a chill clawed at Edjeera's extremities. She found herself shivering, though she knew not if it was from the cold or fear. Scanning the gray, opaque horizon around her, she searched for a shadow or a hazy blotch that might give the rider's position away. She cursed her own breathing, a sound that seemed to reverberate in the stillness and interfered with her searching ears. Geda's hooves crunched on the loose rocks and dead grass so that even her softest steps could be heard in the quiet. Edjeera spurred Geda to move more quickly and erratically. It worsened the noise from Geda's hooves, but if they moved fast enough, the rider should have trouble shooting her, especially in this fog. In one hand, she clutched Geda's reins and a chosen arrow against her palm, and in the other, she rested her bow and two additional arrows on her hip.

A shadow rose out of the mist and spooked Edjeera, but it was too small to be a horse and rider. As Geda trotted closer, the shadow transformed into a pole with a skull resting atop. Two long horns rose from the skull's forehead, as the horns of an antelope might. But the forehead was too large, too rounded to be any hoofed animal that Edjeera knew. She hadn't noticed these ornaments when she was last here, so absorbed in her fear she was. They must have been skulls of the horned invaders the Koureki had slain so long ago, which now stood as warnings.

She heard the crunch of hooves against rock to her left and turned to see a much larger shadow sweeping through the mists. She told Geda to make a sharp turn, but an arrow whistled between her head and Geda's. The wind that followed the missile slammed into her at the same time her shock did. She cursed herself for being careless. Had the horse been a little slower or faster, the arrow would have hit either Geda or her.

Edjeera whirled to her left to pursue the rider. The shadow was gone, but she could still hear the muffled clomp, clomp, clomp echoing through the damp. Her eyes narrowed, searching the fog for the rider's shadow.

There it was. Another arrow flew through the place she had just been and Edjeera stretched her own bow and fired into the mists before the shadow could disappear. As the arrow vanished, she realized that unless the rider or its horse made some cry of pain, she might never know if she hit it. This thought was dashed as soon as she heard the arrow clatter against the stony ground. She had missed.

The shadow disappeared again and Edjeera tried to follow it. She kept Geda's path erratic and unpredictable. It saved her life again. Twice an arrow flew from the mist and struck the area Edjeera would have been had she maintained a straight line.

When the shadow next reappeared, she was able to launch another shot. But her second arrow met the same fate as the first and clattered to an inglorious end.

Edjeera's mind began to race. The rider might have a bottomless quiver, but she did not, and this game would exhaust her supply quickly. She needed another way to fight this demon.

A clatter of hooves to her right made Edjeera turn and another arrow shot past her. She saw a shadow and raced toward it without weaving, hoping she might be able to ride close enough to fire a clean shot. She was rewarded when the shadow did not disappear. Instead, it grew larger, too large to be a rider and horse. Edjeera startled as she drew face-to-face with a massive, bony monster. She whirled Geda about to avoid running into the creature, but when she turned back, she realized the monster was just a massive skeleton. Its skull rivaled Edjeera's own body in size, and two tusks–each the length of Geda–emerged from around the dead beast's mouth. The creature's ribcage lay half-embedded in the ground, as if the very dirt was devouring it.

The creature had been one of the great beasts that the horned-men had ridden when they invaded long ago. Edjeera circled the skeleton, judging to see if it could provide some use to her. As she did so, she heard the sound of hooves behind her.

She whirled Geda about in time to see an arrow fly past her. The rider was no longer a shadow this time and she could make out its features clearly. Perhaps it too had grown tired of blindly launching arrows at her.

This was her chance and she leveled her arrow at the spirit. The rider hunched low against its horse to make itself a smaller target, and turned to outrace her aim and disappear back into the mists. She had to make this shot. It was her best chance of finishing this game. However, in her haste, Edjeera aimed at the rider, not where the rider would be when the arrow arrived. She cursed her stupidity as the arrow scraped uselessly on the stony floor.

Now, the rider was gone again, although she could hear it circling her. Edjeera checked her quiver and made a quick count of her remaining arrows, but she was distracted as something small and furry scrambled out of Geda's way.

Edjeera heard a crack below her. Geda screamed and Edjeera slammed into her mount's neck. Her horse buckled and the ground came rushing up to Edjeera. She still wasn't sure what had happened, but her mount was collapsing. Quickly untangling her feet from the saddle, she leapt from Geda's back before her legs became trapped under the horse's bulk. She tried to roll but instead splayed and skidded across the dirt and stony ground. While shielding her head as well as possible, Edjeera felt her hands take the worst of the fall.

Her head swam. Her arms, thighs and palms throbbed like her beating heart. Salty blood welled up warmly against her bitten tongue. But she rolled onto her back and forced herself to sit up. Geda writhed and screamed with a sound that threatened to shake Edjeera into pieces. She found she couldn't concentrate because of the horse's wail. That terrible scream filled her mind and drowned her thoughts.

She saw little rodents standing like people nearby, with black, marble eyes wide as they regarded Geda and Edjeera with curious terror.

Edjeera felt the ground shake beneath her and fear compelled her to rise. She couldn't hear the hoofbeats, but she felt the ground thump with their approach. She careened to her feet and sought out from where the rider was coming. Edjeera did not spy the spirit, but she did spy the bones of the great horned beast. Instinctively, she charged toward it but stumbled to her knees. She noticed her bow lying beside her and snatched it before racing toward the beast again. Her gait was a wobble and each step of her left foot shot an electric jolt up her leg. At any moment, she expected an arrow to pierce her back, or for the shadow to ride her down and cut her as if she were a stalk of wheat.

When she reached the skeleton, still un-pierced, Edjeera slid onto her stomach, crawled beneath the skull of the beast and emerged within its rib cage. If the rider wanted to shoot or strike her, it would have to ride close to the skeleton, allowing her to strike back.

But she could only strike if she could maintain her composure. Rather than crouch with arrow notched, she sat with her back against the skull, limply clutching the bow, and trying to take in ragged, gasping breaths. Her heart raced, she wheezed through dry lips, and Geda screamed. Geda had been wailing the entire time and she would not stop screaming. Edjeera fought back the tears, but her courage was failing. She wanted to go back to Kourek; she wanted this nightmare to end. If she had never left the city, if she hadn't followed the rider to earn her role of Varza, Geda would not be suffering as she was now.

Edjeera realized that she would die here, in this crater. Perhaps the spirit hadn't been a test. It had been a punishment. The spirit was her executioner. She thought of how, perhaps the next day, a Koureki rider would venture forth when she hadn't come back. He would find her body, bloody and broken, and bring the limp thing back to Kourek. There, Tanjiati would lament at her passing, her father would shake his head at her failure, and her mother and sisters would weep.

"I'm sorry," she choked out between sobs. "I'm so, so sorry."

She did not know if she said this to Geda, or her family, or Tanjiati, or even herself. Perhaps it was a shared atonement.

An arrow smashed into one of the beast's ribs and became stuck, with the arrowhead protruding a hand's length from Edjeera's head. Chips of bone battered her face as the impact shook her into lucidity. The spirit rode toward the skeleton, with its mount's thundering hoofs shaking her very bones. The rider circled around the rear of the beast, behind its backbone, and emerged on the other side, reaching for another arrow in its quiver. Edjeera flattened herself against the ground as another arrow flew at her. This one ricocheted off a rib, flew through her cage, and smacked a rib on the opposite side before clattering onto the ground.

The rider disappeared from view around the head of the beast and Edjeera pushed herself to her knees. She was not in her beloved city. She was not surrounded by her family, or Tanjiati, or her people. Geda was in torturous pain. She had chosen this path and now needed to face its consequences.

She checked her quiver, but most of her arrows were broken, cracked or bent from the fall. Edjeera chose one that looked straight enough to fly and notched it. When the rider reappeared, she shot at the spirit from between two ribs. The arrow never had a chance of hitting the spirit. It spiraled away from its target into the mists. The rider retreated and Edjeera could only follow it by its shadow.

Edjeera took the moment to pull out her splintered arrows. Only three remained in worthy shape. Three chances to kill the rider. Her sword had disappeared from her belt and when she looked out from her cage, she saw it, still hilted, lying beside a writhing Geda. The horse lay in the dirt, her beautiful coat matted with soil and dead grass. One leg was bent in an odd fashion, and Edjeera realized Geda had broken her foot. Edjeera swore an oath when she realized the reason. Several rodents stood on their hind legs, watching the horse from a safe distance. Their scolding chitters could be heard in the brief moments when Geda paused to take a breath before screaming again. Edjeera couldn't see the rodents' holes from here, but Geda must have stepped in one as they ran blindly through the mists, just as the Tichnik's horses had so long ago.

Edjeera considered killing her mount, shooting away the pain, but as she notched an arrow, she remembered that she only had three left. She couldn't spare the missile. Edjeera screamed her own frustration and shielded her eyes against Geda's agony. But she could not hide from the agonizing noise and her piercing guilt.

The only way she could spare Geda her pain would be to kill the spirit. She saw Geda in her mind. She saw Tanjiati. She saw Jurkarthi's bloody face. She saw the rider emerge from the mists, and she saw the arrow that flew from its hand. Edjeera shifted, but the arrow bounced off a rib and sprang into the sky to be lost in the mists above her.

She raised her bow and fired her notched arrow. It smashed directly into the rib in front of her, cracking the rib along its entire length. Its fletching wavered a moment in front of her nose as if teasing her. The rider whirled its horse about in order to retreat back into the mists. Edjeera cursed her haste that had led to such a bad shot.

The rider raced around the rear of the beast, not fully engulfed by the mists, but far enough to let it prepare another arrow. Edjeera did the same and raised the fletching tip up to her eye. She noticed the arrowhead wavering in front of her vision, so she tried to breathe deeply to steady her aim. She only had two arrows left. It would not do to lose one to panic. The rider rode close enough that it was no longer a hazy shadow and fired another arrow. This one flew through the ribcage, missing every rib, but also missing Edjeera. Again, the spirit began to retreat. Edjeera exhaled. She checked that there would be no rib in front of her this time. She reminded herself that she only had one more arrow after this one.

When she thought she had a clean shot, she let the arrow fly. It disappeared and Edjeera reached for her last arrow. But the rider's mount collapsed and the spirit tumbled over its head. The spirit landed a horse's span further than its mount, rolling in the stones and dirt.

Edjeera wasted no time. She lowered the bow, scrambled back under the skull, cringing at the pain from her scraped hands and arms. When she emerged, she notched her last arrow, but realized in her rush, she had snapped it. She swore again and flung the bow and arrow pieces to the ground. She sought out her sword and spied it lying by Geda. She raced for it, almost hopping to avoid the lightning pain in her screaming left ankle. Dodging Geda's writhing legs, Edjeera snatched up the sword and searched for where the spirit had fallen.

The spirit remained where it had landed, but it was rising to its feet as she watched, though not without some effort. Three posts with horned-man skulls surrounded the rider like points on a triangle. She did not pause, remembering the dazed state she was in after falling from Geda's back. Edjeera raced over, as best she could with the pain in her twisted ankle. She unsheathed her father's sword, tossed the hilt away and screamed her war cry. The rider's horse lay where it had fallen with Edjeera's arrow stuck in its neck, but the spirit was holding aloft its own sword even as she charged.

The spirit tried to sidestep the swing, but its stance was too narrow and its feet slipped on the stony ground. Instead, it raised its sword to parry, but Edjeera adjusted her swing. Rather than aiming for its head, she would take off its right leg. The spirit moved to parry this swing, too, but its movement was too late and as the two swords collided with each other, Edjeera was able to drive her edge into the spirit's calf. The clash vibrated into her hand and the clank of steel against steel rang through the mists. The spirit did not cry out, though it did stumble backward, nearly pulling the sword from Edjeera's hand.

Edjeera tried to pull the sword free from the spirit's flesh, and the spirit took the opportunity to make a wild swing. She leaned backward, using her weight to dislodge the blade, but her aching ankle prevented her from jumping out of the way of the spirit's sword. The tip sliced into her upper left arm and she gasped as a bolt of lightning shot through her arm.

Pushing through the pain, Edjeera recovered herself and paused to consider how best to strike next. The spirit took the moment to steady itself, too. It did not whimper from the pain in its leg, but it clearly placed most of its weight on the left foot. She also realized that it cradled its left arm to its belly and held its sword in its right hand only. It couldn't seem to raise the left arm and Edjeera wondered if it had been damaged in the fall.

She took a tender step to her left and the spirit countered her. They circled each other a moment, with trembling swords aimed at each other's faces and taking care not to place too much weight on their injured legs. A circlet of burrowing rats surrounded them at a safe distance, bobbing up and down, and scolding the duelists for trespassing on their home.

Edjeera and the spirit teased each other, faking strikes or jabbing at their opponents' faces. But Edjeera's breathing was heavy and every muscle ached.

As they circled, Geda entered her view. The horse still neighed, but its cries were now whimpers rather than the ear-splitting screams from before. She had given up moving and instead begged for release.

Edjeera's guard dropped at the dismal sight and the spirit was quick to take advantage. It slashed at her. She tried to sidestep the swing, but she knew that her twisted ankle prevented her from swift movement, so she parried as well. But the strike was a fake, and the spirit twisted its aim to slash at her thigh.

She cried out as the steel bit her flesh, but she swung back in a wide arc, not to hit but merely to give her room. The spirit jumped back and tried to strike again, but the blade was poorly aimed and it struck one of the poles instead. The skull of the horned man flew off its perch in a graceful arc and clattered onto the stony ground.

Edjeera slashed downward at the spirit. It managed to dodge her blade but left its sword stuck in the pole. This was Edjeera's chance, so she seized it.

She swung upward with all the force that the pain from her injuries allowed. While the spirit barely dodged her blow, her blade sliced the tip of its hood in two, splitting it open and casting light upon the thing's face. Edjeera expected to see the same mess of gristle that she had seen before. Instead, she saw herself. It was a pale, bloodless and nose-less version of herself, but she recognized the shape of her eyes and her square cheekbones and chin. She was completely bald, as if the spirit had taken a razor to her head, but the scalp did not shine. The spirit did not smile or frown, did not show anger or fear; its face was a placid, unreadable block, as if it were a stone mask carved in her likeness.

The shock from the reveal took Edjeera off guard, and she paused a moment too long. The spirit dug its heel into the dirt and launched itself at her. Edjeera tried to aim her blade, but her reaction was too slow and the spirit collided with her. They lurched backward, the spirit falling atop Edjeera.

They landed hard and Edjeera dropped her sword. Her head hit something soft and hairy. The spirit reached for her neck with its unbroken hand and clasped its fingers around it. Edjeera gagged from its grip, and she splayed her own hands upward, searching for something with which she could fight back. She clutched at the spirit's own neck, but it did not seem fazed and only squeezed harder. The world began to spin and Edjeera gasped, her lungs desperate for air. She reached her hands around her, searching for the sword, but found something soft and slightly malleable. She realized it was the spirit's horse that her head now rested on. Her other hand gripped something hard, cold and rough.

She swung the stone into the side of the spirit's head, denting her own rotting face further. She did this twice more before the spirit let go and retreated out of her reach. Edjeera tossed the stone at the spirit's face and it bounced off, nearly bouncing back at Edjeera. She grunted as she heaved herself to a more upright position, coughing as her lungs choked down the welcome air. Out of the corner of her eye, she saw the spirit reach for her father's sword. She searched for the spirit's own sword, but it remained stuck in the pole, beyond her reach. All she had now were rocks and the dead horse she lay against. As the spirit stepped toward her, Edjeera's racing mind remembered she had one other weapon close at hand.

She turned around and reached for her arrow, the one that had felled the horse. It took two tugs, but she managed to pull it free and turned back just as the spirit was raising her father's sword above its head. Before it could swing the blade down, Edjeera cried a last wordless yell and plunged the shaft into the spirit's side where the armor was weak.

The spirit dropped the sword and it clattered onto the rocks. Its knees soon followed, landing with a thud. The spirit's face remained placid, but its body hung limp. It looked at the arrow in its side as if fascinated.

Edjeera did not hesitate and she heaved herself up so she could reach for the sword. She turned the blade to deliver the last blow, but the spirit caught the blade with its hand. Edjeera could see where the steel bit into the spirit's hand, but no blood ran forth. She yanked on the sword, but the spirit held it tightly. It looked at Edjeera with her own eyes, and they stared at each other for a brief moment before the spirit's face began to ripple and mold itself into the same mess of gristle that had been Jurkarthi's ruined visage. But it wasn't Jurkarthi's face; it was her own. Edjeera stared that face down, the one that had plagued her nightmares ever since that fateful day. Instead of balking at the image, she yanked at the sword. The spirit still refused to let go, but this time it guided the tip toward its left breast. Edjeera understood. With what strength remained in her, she plunged the tip, cutting through the leather armor and piercing the spirit's heart.

Its skin cracked and pieces tore from its body like bits of dust catching in the wind. First, its arms, then head, then torso, cape and legs disintegrated into a thousand fluttering pieces like a cloud of black butterflies. Edjeera's arrow tumbled from its perch and her sword felt heavy without the spirit's body to support it. The pieces gathered around her open wounds, scraped palms and her twisted ankle, and they tickled her like hundreds of Tanjiati's kisses. She swiped at them at first, fearful this might be some new tactic from her mysterious foe, but as they became absorbed into her messy wounds, her skin healed and her pain fled. Instead, she was filled with a soothing energy, as if she had just woken up from a long nap.

When her pain was gone and wounds healed, the cloud drifted away from her and joined a larger cloud that Edjeera belatedly realized was the pieces of the spirit's horse. They fluttered toward Geda and surrounded the poor beast in a haze of black particles. When they left, Edjeera rejoiced as she watched Geda rise from the ground, her leg no longer broken.

The cloud then drifted away from Geda to hover for a moment before condensing itself so tight it formed an object that fell to the ground. When Edjeera had enough strength to investigate the object, she found a mask lying there: a mask of a Varza.

It was as black as the spirit and glossy as precious stone, with etchings so small and intricate that a mortal could not have carved them. Dark feathers seamlessly emerged from the forehead, and rows of multi-hued beads hung from strings along its edges. Bits of gold and silver were embedded into the mask's surface, as if it were dotted with stars. As Edjeera looked closer, she realized the carvings depicted her own story, from her flight in the crater to her victory over the spirit.

A drop fell upon it, and she realized that it was not rain, but one of her own tears. With tender hands, she reached for the mask, the trophy that she had desired since she was first able to clutch a wooden sword. Now, after years of watching others place the sacred piece upon their faces, she held it in her hands. Then she pressed it to her heart, cradling it as if it were a child.

She led Geda out of the crater. The horse seemed fully healed, escaping with not even a limp. She seemed in even better vitality than when she entered the crater. That seemed like days ago. But when they emerged from the mists and crested the tops of the hills, the sun was just setting.

It was a clear night and the great moon, with no piece of it missing, painted the world with a pale light so bright that Edjeera could see even the most distant hills clearly. The wind washed over the scene and the grasses cheered Edjeera as she and Geda walked through them. The crickets fell silent at her approach, as if in respect for the victorious warrior. The stars above, sprinkled like little holes in a blanket that covered the sky from horizon to horizon, danced in joyous celebration.

Edjeera led Geda in the direction of Kourek for a time, but the joy locked inside her pressed against her chest. She deviated from the path and raced Geda over the hills, hollering her victory to the night. She stood up in the saddle and let Geda lead herself. She laughed as the wind caught in her hair, and she spread her arms wide as if to hug the sky.

After a time, she paused Geda and dismounted. Edjeera let the horse wander, while she danced and leapt with an exhilaration she had never before felt, and may never feel again. It was a feeling of victory, of weariness, of satisfaction and of completeness, and it could not be contained any longer.

When she finally collapsed, she simply sat beneath the moon watching Geda nibble at grass blades. There was no fear, just tranquil bliss. When this feeling too passed, she took Geda by the reins and led the loyal creature towards home.

Edjeera walked instead of riding most of the way, and so they neared the gates of Kourek with the break of dawn. Though her feet and legs were sore from the hike, she leapt upon Geda and galloped down to the very gates of the city and shouted her presence.

“Who are you? What is your purpose?” demanded the gate guard standing atop the closest tower.

“I am Edjeera!” she proclaimed and held up her mask. “I am Varza!”

Acknowledgements

To make art and display it requires collaboration, and this novella is no different. The product would not be what it is today without the help of my editors, Rik Paul and Yudong Liu; my Beta Readers, Barbara McCole, Tara Paul and Hyungjin Park; and my cover artist, Alison Keller. Thank you all for your hard work in helping me create *Mask of the Varza*.

About the Author

Let me tell you the tale of Nathan Lawrence Paul, author of the *Mask of the Varza*. He is a storyteller from the land of New York with a fascination for history and historical fantasy. He has previously walked the path of photographer and videographer, and both masks influence his writing style. Although Nathan's released stories are not substantial (*Mask of the Varza* is his debut novella), he has one more novella finished and several more partly completed stories. More will be forthcoming.

For tidings, please follow him on Instagram at @nathanlpaul.

www.ingramcontent.com/pod-product-compliance
Lightning Source LLC
LaVergne TN
LVHW090617110826
845146LV00001B/432